POUNDED BY THE POMMEL HORSE

SABRINA CROSS

Copyright ©2024 by Sabrina Cross

All Rights Reserved.

The characters and events portrayed in this book are fictitious. Any similarity to real persons, living or dead, is coincidental and not intended by the author.

No part of this book may be reproduced, or stored in a retrieval system, or transmitted in any form or by any means, electronic, mechanical, photocopying, recording, or otherwise without express written permission of the copyright owner. For permission requests, email authorsabrinacross@gmail.com

Edited by: Writer's Wingman

Cover Design: Sabrina Cross

This book is 100% human made. No generative AI was used in the writing, editing, or production of this book. We support human artists in this house.

 Formatted with Vellum

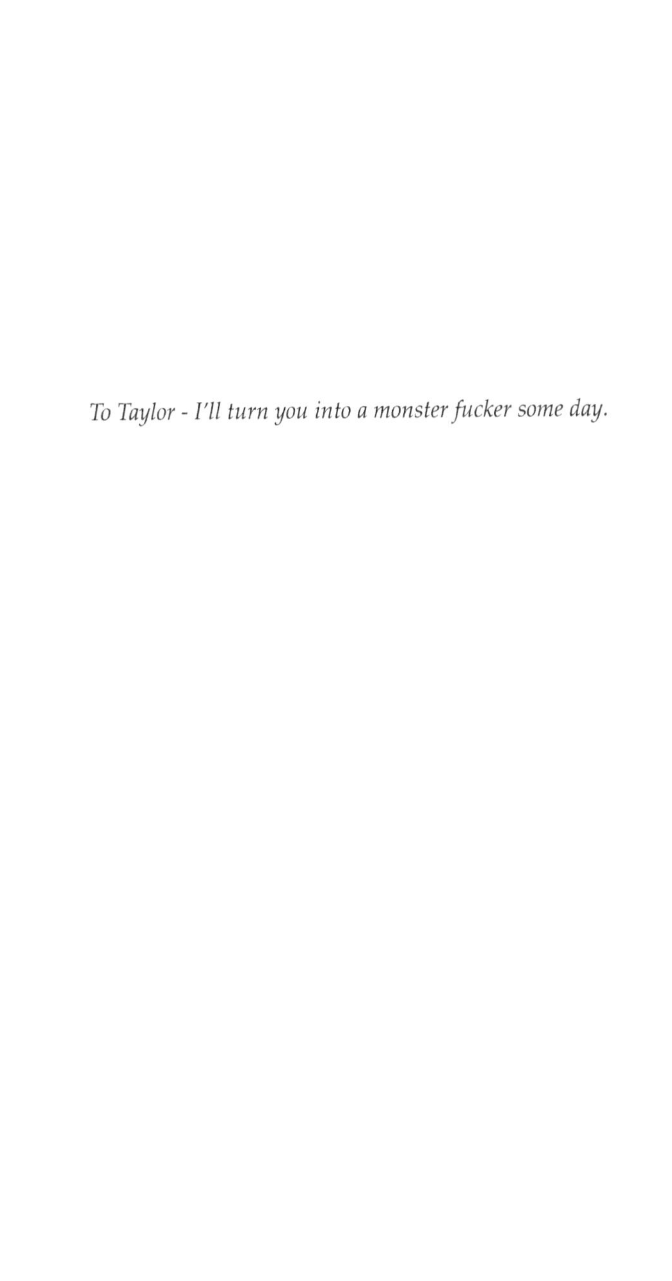

To Taylor - I'll turn you into a monster fucker some day.

AUTHOR'S NOTE

This is a sentient object romance. Humans will be getting it on with sentient objects. Don't worry, everyone is gleefully consenting.

If you read the last three sentences and think that's not for you, that's okay. There is still time to put this book down and walk away. No one will blame you. It's the sane thing to do.

But if you're going to stick around please be aware of the following: This book has dub-con with a semi-sentient object (but the object doesn't object). There is graphic sex (Oral, vaginal), graphic language.

If you feel I am missing anything please reach out to me at authorsabrinacross@gmail.com and let me know. A complete list can be found at www.sabrinacross.com

CHAPTER 1
ELENA

And once again, ladies and gents, Elena Brown takes the lead!" My best friend and teammate, Sophia announced loudly as the electronic board rankings were updated.

The board showed the top ten gymnasts at the Michigan Elite Gymnastics Club rankings and most recent scores.

For years, I had been competing against Bryson Lorn for the top spot. He and I almost always scored the highest rankings among our teams, but the top spot at the gym flipped back and forth depending on who had a better day.

Today, I was on top.

Just like he asked me to be the night before while seriously drunk and stupid. We'd walked down that path once before and the experience had been...underwhelming to say the least.

I looked around the space to catch Bryson's reaction but he was nowhere to be seen. Probably somewhere with his head in a trash can, based on the level of drunk he'd appeared when he gave me the less than tempting suggestion to 'hop on his cock.'

My workout was brutal that day and I found

myself practically limping off the mats when I, unfortunately, ran into Bryson. He looked a little worse for the wear, his sweat-soaked face was practically green.

"Hey Bry, you look like shit."

"Fuck you." Well, okay then. I went to pass by him but he stopped me with a hand

on my arm. "Don't get too comfortable with that top spot. It'll be mine again soon enough."

"Maybe, maybe not." I shook my arm loose. "It's okay, Bry-bry. Some men just peak early."

He moved to stand in front of me, blocking my path to the locker rooms. I wasn't worried,

there were still plenty of people in the gym. Besides, Bryson was a lot of things but he'd never been the violent type.

"The only reason you've been on top this long is because girl's gymnastics is easier than men's. You wouldn't last a day doing what I do."

I raised an eyebrow at him. "Sexist much?"

I turned around and crossed the gym to escape him. I wasn't in the mood to entertain his

bullshit. I would just go out the side door and circle back around. When I neared the pommel horses, Bryson stopped me again.

"I bet you that you can't do a full routine on one of these." He patted a pommel horse next to us.

"Pretty sure I could. But you couldn't do an artistic routine on the floor. Men are all power moves, they don't have the grace and agility to do it."

"Bet."

CHAPTER 2
POM

was tired of being used.

I wanted so much more than to be some tool for the unwashed men that used me day in and day out. Truth be told, I wanted nothing more than to tell the men off and go on about my life. But I wasn't ready. Not yet.

Though, I wasn't sure exactly what it was I needed to be ready. I knew I was getting stronger and stronger every day, closer to the moment I would be able to get up and leave my servitude. There was just something missing, some element I hadn't yet been exposed to that would complete my transition.

Strong, solid hands slammed onto my back and I shuddered under the blow. Once, I hadn't been alert enough to feel pain. Once, that action would have elicited no response. But now, I just marked it down as another reason for my revenge.

"You've got no shot. Women don't have the strength to do the horse." Ugh, I knew that voice. Bryson Lorn. He was one of the most insufferable humans I was forced to suffer though. He was rough and vulgar. My revenge would start with him.

"We'll see." The voice was like nothing I'd ever heard before. Sweet and lilting, it had every nerve in my body on attention. "Tomorrow. 5am before everyone else shows up."

"I can't wait to watch you fall on that tight little ass. Just like you'll be falling on my cock when I dominate the floor tomorrow." I bit back a gagging noise. The person Bryson was talking to did not.

"Even if I fall on my head and develop amnesia, there's nothing that will get me to go near your syphilis-infested cock."

"We'll see." Bryson said. The voices faded away and soon everything was silent. This was my favorite part of the day. The time when all of the humans had gone and I could really become. What I was becoming was still a little unclear but I was definitely changing. Soon, soon I would find the missing piece and be able to free myself from the indignities of the gym..

I was just settling into my late night meditations when it happened. It shot through me like lightning and I could feel every cell in my body come to life. I was practically vibrating with the feel of it.

No, wait. I really was vibrating.

Someone was using me. I could feel the tug on my pummels, the heavy weight on my back. Though not as heavy as it usually was.

There was something different about this time. Something amazing.

Excitement zinged through me like lightening.

It was coming. Whatever it was that I needed, it was here. I was close.

I would become.

CHAPTER 3
ELENA

came down hard with the pommel horse between my legs. I caught one of the handles and controlled my skid. I used my grip to pull myself forward, rather than slip off of the side of the horse. Again.

A shock of sensation cut through me when my clit scraped against the leather. My lower lips splayed wide in my shorts, exposing the bundle of nerves to the back of the horse. Before I could think about it, I was repeating the movement. Rubbing my needy cunt against the worn leather of the equipment. I'd done three or four more frantic thrusts before I caught myself.

What the hell was I doing? Sure, it'd been a long time since I'd been with someone but I'd never once considered humping gym equipment.

I looked around the dark space. No one was here, I'd bypassed the security system when I came in so the cameras would be off. No one would ever know. I slowly circled my hips, dragging my sensitive clit along the firm bar between my legs.

Maybe a part of me was even turned on by the fact I was so out in the open and exposed. I thought about what would happen if someone walked in and saw me rubbing myself on the back of the pommel horse like a whore in heat. Would they mock me? Get off to watching me? Maybe they would ask to join me. Or maybe they'd tell me exactly what to do. I'd have no choice but to obey because they'd be able to hold my indiscretion over my head.

I moved faster to the thought. Tugging one breast out of the top of my sports bra so I could pull on my rock hard nipple. Alternating between pinching and pulling and rolling the bud as I moved my hips along the horse.

"This is so fucked up." I muttered as I neared the edge. My pants and moaned echoed loudly in the empty space, bouncing around in the dark gym.

Still, no matter how fucked up it was, I was going to come. I could feel my orgasm building up inside of me. It was so good it felt like the ground was shaking beneath me. And when the wave finally crashed, I could do nothing but hold on and ride.

CHAPTER 4
POM

his was it. Warm liquid seeped into my flesh and I could feel the spark of life that I had been missing.Fire and ice ran through me. There was agony like I'd never experienced before. My body contorted, stretching, shrinking, breaking, and mending. So many sensations ripped through me.

I was at last being born into my true self.

A scream echoed off the walls as the weight of the human fell off of me. I would worry about her in a moment. First, I needed to finish my transformation.

The pain slowly abated as I lay panting on the ground. Oxygen seared its way to my newly formed lungs. My pulse was a drumbeat throughout my body. It was strange but I felt stronger than ever before, even as I fought for strength to move.

"What, what, how, the fuck?" The female's voice was high and hurt my ears. I reached up and touched the side of my head. I did have ears. How wonderful.

"Don't worry." The words were a rasp of sound.

I cleared my throat and tried again. "Don't worry, I won't hurt you."

I pushed myself to roll over so I could look upon the face of the woman who had sparked my change. She was beautiful. Dark hair framed a face that seemed to be made up of giant dark eyes and a wide mouth. Oh, wait, no, the mouth was gaping. It probably didn't always look like that.

"What the actual fuck?"

"I do not believe there has been an actual fuck. Did what you did to me count as a fuck?"

"No. No, no, no, no no. This is not happening." The girl shook her head and backed away from me slowly. Something in my gut (I had a gut!) told me to stop her. There was something special about this human and I wanted to figure out what it was.

I lurched to my feet, unsteady and stumbling, and reached out to take her arm.

"Please, don't leave. I mean you no harm." I attempted a smile but it only seemed to scare her more. "I could never harm you. You are the one who gave me life."

"Wha-what?" She was shaking under my hand and I wished to soothe her nerves.

"Shhhh." I brushed a hand down the side of her head in a gentle motion, loving the softness of her hair. So many new sensations and I wanted to experience them all.

CHAPTER 5
ELENA

here was a naked man in the gym. There was a naked man that used to be a pommel horse. A pommel horse that I'd just used as a sex toy.

Oh my god. Oh my god. Oh my god.

"I'm hallucinating. That's the only explanation. I fell and hit my head and now I have a brain bleed and I'm hallucinating."

That was the only reasonable option. Because there was no way I was talking to a man who used to be a pommel horse. That didn't happen. That wasn't a real thing.

Besides, I couldn't have dreamed up a better looking man if I tried. He was a giant man, tall, and lean, and easily a foot-and-a-half taller than my five-four. His hair was a dirty blond and his eyes stormy sea blue. His body was a wonderland of ridges and ripples. An insane part of me wanted to run my tongue up the cleft in his chin. He was perfect wank material.

"Be gentle," he said, petting my hair like I was a skittish cat. "You're safe with me."

Something nudged my hip and I looked down

to see his cock rising to full-mast. I jumped away from him.

"Okay, hey, no. No, buddy. Put that thing away." I spun around, looking for something, anything to put on him. I spotted an abandoned hot pink sweatshirt and rushed to grab it. I returned to shove the balled up jacket at random dude's doodle and berries.

"This is…soft? Yes, soft. I like this." He raised the jacket up and brought it to rub against his cheek.

Okay, and yes, I probably should be worried about the clear head wound that caused this hallucination. Or I should be more concerned about the aroused man currently cuddling a hot pink hoodie. But I was strangely calm about the whole thing. I didn't feel threatened and fuck knew I liked looking at him. It didn't matter that he was either a hallucination, insane, or the actual fucking pommel horse, I felt comfortable with him.

"Feel!" He pressed the sweatshirt to my face and I yelped and backed away. I wasn't sure who the hoodie belonged to but it stank of perfume. Like the whole bottle had spilled on it. And while it was soft, it was still a hoodie being shoved against my face and suffocating me.

"Okay, yeah, no. Normal people don't shove sweatshirts into complete stranger's faces."

"But I am not a normal person." He hugged the sweatshirt close and his face was closed off with drawn eyes and firm lips.

"What are you?"

"I'm not sure. I was that." He pointed at the pommel horses nearby. "But for a long time now I've been becoming more. And now I am this."

He spread his arms wide, giving me an uninterrupted view of his eight-pack abs and impressive package.

I was an elite gymnast. I was used to physically fit and attractive guys. None of the dudes at the gym had anything on this guy. Again, I was struck with the urge to lick him. This time I wanted to trace the dip at his hip and the muscles that lead inward like an arrow to his cock.

The thought had me getting wet as I imagined what could happen if I did just drop to my knees and lick a path to his dick before taking him into my mouth.

Okay, well, that wasn't like me. I didn't often sexualize men I just met. But there was something about this one that kept sending my brain into the gutter.

"Assuming I'm not hallucinating, how are you like this?"

CHAPTER 6
POM

S uch a simple and complicated question. I honestly didn't have a clue how I'd become this form. I knew with every drop of blood, sweat, and tears from the men who used me, I became more aware. I could hear and sense people around me. I could smell the usually pungent odor of sweaty men.

Then there was the knowing. I knew things I shouldn't know, felt things a piece of gym equipment shouldn't be able to feel. The more I was exposed to people the more I seemed to understand them. I could name my body parts without ever having a body before.

But how did you explain simply becoming and knowing? It seemed fantastical. Then again, an hour ago I had been a pommel horse and now here I was in a skin suit.

I took a deep breath and froze. There was something new. Something salty and earthy that had my cock standing at attention and my hair on end. I sniffed again, moving nearer to the woman who had stopped cowering. She took a step back.

"Woah, buddy. You stay away from me with that thing." She waved somewhere around my waist and I realized it was my cock that was making her uncomfortable. I took the soft bundle of fabric and covered the area with it. But I couldn't stop myself from taking another step forward, trying to figure out the source of the scent.

My mouth was watering as I fell to my knees and wrapped my arms around her legs to keep her in place. I followed the smell to the source, between her legs and buried my face there.

"Eep!" She pushed at my head. "What the fuck are you doing?"

"Smells so good." I nuzzled into her, trying to cover myself in the delightful smell. "I want to drown in it."

"No. Nope. You need to stop that right now." Her voice was high pitched and she grabbed a handful of my hair and yanked, pulling me away from her. "First rule of humans, you don't stick your face between their legs like a fucking dog."

Her face was red and she looked very distressed. I released her to rub my hands over her sides.

"Okay. What do you do? I need more of that smell. I need to taste it." The red on her face got darker and her breathing was coming out too fast. I was worried for her. That couldn't be normal.

We stayed there for what felt like a very long time. Some of the color left her face and her breathing slowed to something more normal. I continued to stroke her body, down her sides, over her hips, up and down her legs. Her skin was so soft, little bumps and lines giving it an interesting texture. I could spend forever touching her.

"Okay," she said suddenly, breaking the silence. "You can taste it."

I immediately shoved my face back toward the source, sliding my tongue out to try to get a taste of the delicious scent. I only got the taste of cotton before the girl pulled me back by my hair.

"No, not like that." She released my hair and began playing with the hem of her shirt. "I can't believe I'm doing this."

"You're not doing anything. You're standing there while I feast. What do you have to do?"

CHAPTER 7
ELENA

sighed but was smiling. For someone who knew a surprising amount of things, he was so totally clueless about others.

"Look, actually, I don't know your name. I should know it. It's something a girl should know before letting a guy go down on her."

The man remained on his knees before me, his large hands gripping my hips like he was afraid I would run.

I probably should. The connection I feel to this man makes no sense. But I can't help but feel comfortable around him. Well, not exactly comfortable. I was insanely turned on by him and was still embarrassed I smelled to strongly he knew I was wet for him.

"I don't have a name. Call me whatever you like." He tried to stick his face between my legs again and I stopped him with a hand on his forehead.

"You need a name!"

"I'm Pommel." He shrugged.

"I can't call you Pommel! How about Pom? Can I call you Pom?" He nodded vigorously.

"Yes, please. Can I taste you now?"

I'd never had a guy so eager to go down on me before and it was a heady feeling. Normally oral sex with men was very transactional. A guy spent the minimum effort down there before expecting me to return the favor. Pom wasn't asking for me to do anything for him but seemed genuinely needy for my cunt.

I released his head and he dove back in, licking me over my shorts. I jerked in response but it was more surprise than sensation.

Was I really going to do this? Let a complete stranger eat me?

I looked down into his stormy blue eyes and decided yes, yes I was. He looked like a kicked puppy, like he would cry if he didn't get access to my pussy. If he had been forceful I wouldn't have even considered it but he stopped without complaint over and over again.

"You'll have better luck if you take my pants off." The words were barely out of my mouth before he was yanking my shorts down my legs. He left them at my ankles and shoved his face between my legs again.

I laughed as I fought to fight my feet free of the restraining material before I fell over. Not that I was super concerned about falling with the tight grip Pom had on my hips. I finally worked one leg free and was able to spread my legs a little for him.

His tongue shot out and licked over my wet folds and he groaned against me. I shuddered in response to the vibration just over my clit. He kept lapping at me, his tongue driving its way between my folds to lick at my clit and vulva. It was awkward and honestly a little annoying. I wanted to compare him to a dog again but given the context, I refused to let my brain complete the thought.

"Can I just…" I pulled his head away using his hair. "Let me show you."

"Show me what?" So sincere. I wondered if he knew what pleasure was.

"How to make it good for the both of us." I grabbed his hands and pulled them off of my hips so I could lower myself to the mats. Honestly, it was not the best place to be laying but I didn't want to wait and I wasn't sure Pom would let me take him anywhere else. His expression was practically feral.

I spread my legs, leaving them bent at the knees with my feet planted on the mat. I propped myself up on one elbow and brought one hand to my pussy.

"You can lick and suck here."

I moved my fingers down and inserted two of them into my hole.

"You can lick and touch here. This is where the scent comes from."

"I think I got it." Pom said, he drew my hand away from my body and pressed it to my belly. He moved to lay on his stomach on the mats and then he was there, his face between my legs. He licked a path from my clit to my hole. Over and over again, the same motion.

"Suck my clit." I begged. I needed more sensation.

He did, hard. My body bowed up.

"Too hard, too much!" He lowered the suction. He drew my clit into his mouth in rhythmic motions. At the same time he brought his fingers into it, pushing two into me. His fingers were a heck of a lot bigger than mine and it was a tight fit.

"You're so warm and wet here." He pulled his fingers out to look at them. They glistened with my cream. He eyed them for a moment before putting his fingers in his mouth.

He groaned around them. "You taste better than you smell."

His fingers returned to my vagina, enough for a couple thrusts before pulling out again. I nearly whined. My body was on edge.

Pom shocked me when he brought his fingers up to my mouth and forced their way in.

"Taste." He demanded. I could do nothing but obey.

I'd never tasted myself like this before. Sure, I'd kissed a guy after he went down on me but having his fingers in my mouth simply to taste myself was something different. It felt filthy. But as I swirled my tongue around his fingers, I couldn't help but savor the earthy taste.

"Mmm, that feels good." Pom said, pulling his fingers from my mouth only to slide them back into me. His head dipped down and he began licking and sucking at my clit again. Once he found his rhythm, he was shockingly good at something he'd only learned existed just moments before.

He worked me up to the edge until I was writhing and panting on the gym floor, my fingers scrambling for something to hold onto to anchor myself. I was on the verge of flying out of my skin. I'd never had anyone get me to the edge so fast. And that included my ex roommate who ate pussy like it was her job.

I gripped his hair in my hand, desperate for release. He suddenly stopped.

"What? Stop? Please don't make me stop." He begged. I was confused for a moment before I realized what he meant.

"Don't stop. Please. Keep going. I just want to touch your hair. Is that okay?"

"Yes." He reached up and pressed his hand over mine to hold it in place even as he ducked his head back between my legs and continued to consume me. It only took another moment of grinding against his face before I fell off the cliff and was drowning in pleasure.

"Oh, fuck." Pom's utterance cut through the haze of orgasm. I didn't understand what he meant until he pulled his fingers free of me only to replace them with his tongue. He lapped at me like a kitten with a bowl of milk.

His tongue drove into me over and over again, keeping me right on the edge. Pleasure was turning to discomfort as he tasted my overstimulated flesh. His moans and groans vibrated through my body. I wanted more. I wanted it to stop. I wanted him to never stop.

"Oh, oh shit. What?" He suddenly stopped and sat up and stared in horror at his lap. I sat up to see what the problem was and had to slap my palm to my face to keep from laughing.

"I broke something." He said in absolute horror as his cock twitched and spurted. Cum slid down the shaft into the curls at the base.

"No, baby. You came." I shifted and crawled over to him, bending to take his still hard cock in my mouth. He hadn't asked and for some reason, that made me want to suck his cock even more.

I licked up his shaft and stopped, pulling away.

"You taste…" I couldn't place the taste. A little chalky, sweet and sour. I licked him again, trying to place the flavor.

"Is it bad?" I licked again and kept the cum in my mouth as I leaned up to kiss him. His cum slid over our tongues and they tangled.

"Pixie sticks!" I said suddenly, pulling away from him. "You taste like pixie sticks. I haven't had those in years." Sugar was not a part of the diet of an elite gymnast. I'd stopped being allowed to have candy when I was seven. But I could still remember the powdery candy.

"You can have my pixie stick anytime you want." His voice was so earnest, I threw my head back and laughed.

CHAPTER 8
POM

She was beautiful when she laughed. I wanted to drown myself in the sound. I wanted to taste the column of her neck. I wanted to bury myself between her breasts, I wanted to lose every part of myself in her. She made me feel warm and good where before only anger and resentment existed.

I realized something I was missing.

"What do I call you?" I asked. She stopped laughing and her gaze snapped to mine. Her eyes were wide and her mouth slowly formed an O shape.

"Oh, my god. I just let a guy eat me and he doesn't even know my name."

"Is that bad?"

"Yes! I'm such a slut." She seemed on the edge of panic and I wasn't sure what to do about it. I didn't want her to run away from me so I wrapped her in my arms and pulled her onto my lap.

"I'm not sure what a slut is, but I'm sure you're not one if it's bad. You are the opposite of bad. Everything about you is amazing and perfect."

That seemed to make her feel a little better. She

at least stopped fighting me and allowed herself to go still in my arms.

"You are my life. It's only because of you I exist as I am now." I ran my hand over her hair, enjoying the softness of it. I also enjoyed the way her head fell against my chest. Her face was damp against my skin.

"Elena," she whispered. "My name is Elena."

We sat there, with her wrapped in my arms, for what felt like forever and only a moment. The silence of the gym was soothing.

But I still had a more than half naked woman in my arms and my body knew what it wanted to do with her. My soothing strokes began to slide lower to brush across the top of her ass, inward to brush my hands along the sides of her breasts. She began to squirm in my arms, which caused my cock to twitch.

I buried my face in her neck and hair, smelling her skin. I didn't have the words for the smells but I couldn't get enough of them. Her entire body was a sensory delight.

She was beautiful, her skin soft over firm muscle. I could drown myself in the way she smelled. Her cunt was the only taste I wanted on my tongue.

With that thought in mind, I shifted to lay her back down on the floor so I could have another taste. I was starving and she was the only thing I wanted to eat.

"You can't be serious," Elena said as I slid down her body and spread her legs wide. "Really, how much is enough?"

"When it comes to tasting you, I'll never get enough." I dipped my head and ran my tongue through her folds to get a taste of her before moving to suck the little bud that brought her so much pleasure. My cock was hard and I shifted to grind it against the soft floor. The friction made the ache better and worse.

Elena's hand went to my hair and I waited for her to tug me away again. I would probably cry, but I would stop if she demanded it of me. But instead of pulling me away, she pulled my head closer, shoving it into her spread legs. Spread legs that were beginning to shake around my head. Spread legs that had the most delicious nectar in the center.

"Oh, oh, oh, oh my god!" Elena moaned, bowing up into my mouth. I gripped her hips and held her there, giving me better access to her sweet cunt. "Don't stop."

Never.

I would never stop. I needed nothing but the taste of her.

CHAPTER 9
ELENA

was going to die. But lord I would die happy. I had come more times than I could count and still he devoured me like he couldn't get enough. It was good, amazing. But it wasn't enough. I wanted so much more.

I used my grip on his hair to pull his head away. He let out a sound that a less generous person would have called a whine.

"Please." He pulled my hand from his hair and kissed my palm. "I'm not done with you."

Oh god, he was going to kill me.

"Can't." I swallowed against my dry throat. "I cannot possibly."

He let out another whine but dropped my legs from around his shoulders and slowly climbed up my body to lay down next to me. He stretched out alongside me, resting his head on my shoulder. I arched, stretching my sore body. Everything below my waist was completely numb.

"Need water." I croaked, my throat so dry. "It's over there. Can you grab it for me?"

I waved in the general direction of my bag. Pom pushed to his feet and headed toward the side of the mats where I'd dropped my bag when I arrived.

I took a moment to appreciate his ass while he walked away from me.

It was nearly as good as the view as he walked back toward me. His cock was long and hard and standing at attention just begging to be used. I pushed up to my elbows and noted the lack of cum on the mats. How had he not come? He'd forced so many orgasms out of me but hadn't had any release. No wonder it looked so red and angry as he crouched down and handed me the bottle of water.

"What else do you need?" He sounded so concerned and there I was ogling his dick. I wasn't usually the aggressive one in bed. Usually, I preferred going with the flow and let my partner take the lead. But Pom was sweet and so new to pleasure he didn't even know what to ask for.

I downed nearly half of my water bottle before replacing the cap. I reached out for Pom's hand. "Help me up."

He pushed to his feet, dragging me up with him. I gripped his shoulders until I was sure my legs would hold me. They were still shaky from multiple orgasms. I walked over to the nearest pommel horse and patted it. It was about the right height for what I had in mind. I lifted myself up onto it.

"Come here." I said, spreading my legs wide to make room for Pom to stand between them. The position put his mouth nearly level with mine. I wrapped my legs around his thighs and pulled him forward.

Kissing him was so natural and easy. He may have needed a tutorial on eating pussy but kissing appeared to come naturally to him. He kissed me like I was oxygen and he was drowning. He kissed me deep, with long, languid strokes.

He gripped my hips and pulled me close, my

wet and overstimulated cunt rubbed against his torso. The tip of his cock brushed against my ass with every movement. I wiggled against him, needing more and needing a longer break for my sensitive clit.

"Fuck me." I said. I reached down behind me to grab his cock and try to maneuver it inside of me. It was awkward and inelegant but when the tip of his dick notched against my hole, both of us groaned.

"Oh, fuck." Pom groaned into my neck as he slid inside of me in increments. "That feels amazing."

His cock was huge. Larger than any I'd taken before. And that included Monster Cock, the dildo my ex-girlfriend had. My body stretched and burned as he worked his way in. His arms shook as they held me up against the pommel horse. It took me a moment to realize he wasn't struggling with the weight of me but with restraint.

After a few slow moments, his cock was buried deep inside of me. I'd taken all of him but his tip was pressed up against my cervix in a kind of plea-sure pain I'd never experienced before.

It was so good. It was not enough. I needed more.

"Fuck me." I demanded again.

CHAPTER 10
POM

was in heaven and hell. My entire body burned, every muscle was tense, every sensitive nerve had been relocated to my cock. Elena was so tight I could barely work my way into her and now that I was there, I never wanted to leave.

"Fuck me," Elena demanded. She used her feet against my ass to press me forward, deeper into her. She gasped and I froze. My eyes flew to her face. Her head was down, looking at the place we were connected. Her eyes were wide and mouth pulled tight.

I slowly pulled out of her until I was nearly free of her tight hole before pressing back in. I kept my movements slow and easy, not wanting to hurt her.

"I'm not going to break." she told me. Her fingers dug into my shoulders as she tried to move herself. I considered the angles and our heights as I slowly moved her up and down my cock, her weight entirely in my arms. I needed better leverage.

When I pulled out of her entirely, she made a cute little sound and gripped me harder with her legs.

"Shhh, don't worry, baby. I'll give you what you need." Elena didn't look pleased with me but she allowed me to adjust our positions until she was bent over the pummel horse, her ass in the air and wet pussy on display.

"Hold on." I pressed her hands to the handles and pulled her down until I could slide myself back into her heat. It felt like fire branding me, my cock was being strangled. It was exquisite torture and I wanted to spend forever there between her legs.

I gripped her hips and sped up my pace. The sounds she made ramped up my own pleasure. My cock was hard, my balls were high, my skin felt too tight. I held her in place and slammed into her over and over again. I chased the sensation. It was like before, but better. More.

"Yes, Pom, yes. Right there. Harder. Yes." Elena kept up a steady stream of demands

and pleas as I pounded into her. I fucked her hard and fast, my nerves were all on fire.

"Elena, baby, I think I'm coming." I slammed into her one last time before my cock began to spasm, my stomach was clenching and releasing, my legs shook underneath me.

When the sensations faded, I pulled out of Elena, a string of sticky white liquid kept us connected for a long moment.

"No, no, please." Elena's ass was wiggling in the air as she humped against the beam. "I'm so close."

Well, that wouldn't do. I dropped to my knees behind her. I pulled her ass cheeks apart and drove my tongue into her dripping cunt. The taste of her musk and my cum was addictive. She wiggled against my face. Her pants echoed around the dark space as she sought her release.

I slid my hand up her ass to the tight hole there. I pressed gently against it, testing her. She gasped and then moaned again.

"What are you doing?" Her words were breathless and high.

"Fucking you." I told her, pressing my thumb deeper, past the rim of her back hole while I devoured her front hole. I brought my other hand up under to press against her belly so I could use my thumb on her little button. She bucked and moaned against me. She was practically feral as she fucked herself against my face and hands. My thumb pressed deeper and she cried out.

Her body was spasming against me and the beam. I looked up and her hands were gripping the handles hard enough to turn her knuckles white. Her whole body shook and I gently pulled my thumb out of her ass as I gently stroked her clit as she continued to come.

When she was done, I helped her down from the pommel horse and lifted her into my arms. She pressed her lips to my neck. Her body started shaking again and I worried I broke something in her.

It took a moment to realize she was laughing.

"What's so funny?"

"Do you think that one is like you? Did we just traumatize a poor pommel horse?"

"I don't think so." I eyed the piece of equipment carefully, wondering if she was right and there was another being like me so close. "No, I think I'm the only one of my kind."

I lowered us to the mats on the ground, pulling Elena into my lap and keeping her

wrapped up in my arms. Pressing my lips to her hair, I wondered if this was the only time I would be able to have her in my arms. Surely, I could keep her. She was the spark that brought me to life. There had to be a reason for that.

But as we sat there in the silent gym in the middle of the night I couldn't help but feel like she was drifting away from me.

CHAPTER 11
ELENA

o, what happens to you now?" I asked, pulling my shorts on. "Are you like this forever or will you turn back?"

"I don't know," Pom responded, sounding sad.

"Well, what are you going to do?" I fixed my hair back into a messy bun on the top of my head. Pom just sat on the mats, completely naked and at ease, and watched me.

"I don't know."

I pulled my hoodie over my head and went to him. I knelt between his legs and reached out to brush my hand over his hair before I cupped his cheek.

"Will you let me help you?" Pom pressed his hand over mine. The move trapped my hand against his face as he nuzzled into it.

"Will you keep me?" His words were soft and earnest and it pulled on my heart. He sounded so scared and lost.

I had no clue what I was going to do with a man who didn't have a full name, any sort of identification, no job, no understanding of the world at large. My career involved a lot of travel and focus. Boyfriends weren't forbidden but they were definitely discouraged. They were a distraction that I couldn't afford.

But as I sat there looking into his stormy blue eyes I realized I didn't have a choice. I couldn't leave him there. I didn't want to.

Something about Pom called to me, pulled me in. He touched a place inside me that I had never noticed before. Even if he wasn't the best lay I'd ever had in my life, I wouldn't be able to just walk away from him.

"Yes," I pressed my lips to his. "Now, let's find you something to cover your cock so we can go home."

As I took one last look at the gym to make sure I hadn't left any evidence I wondered how I was going to explain the missing pommel horse. There was no way they wouldn't notice the missing four-thousand piece of equipment.

Pom came back wearing a pair of too small joggers he found in the lost and found. I decided I didn't care what they thought happened. I would figure out how to manage the repercussions.

Pom was worth it.

ABOUT THE AUTHOR

Sabrina Cross (she/her) is a neurospicy 80's baby from the middle of nowhere Michigan, where she still lives with her cat. She came into her monster romance era early when she fell in love with Beast from the 1997's X-Men animated series. After discovering sentient object romance in early 2023, Sabrina decided to embrace what she calls her 'Hold My Beer' style of writing and gave into the lifelong dream of being an author. When not writing weird monster/sentient object smut, Sabrina can be found hanging out on social media (@authorsabrinacross), reading, or hoarding office supplies.

ALSO BY SABRINA CROSS

Yarn & Monsters Series

A True Love Spell Gone Wrong...

When four friends perform a true love spell, things go terribly wrong. Now they're locked into a deal with the devil and have only a year to find love and happiness or their souls are destined to face the flames. Armed with a demon guardian; Clover, Jasmine, Fern, and Violet are determined to beat the devil and save themselves. Except, this curse might be the best thing that's ever happened to them.

Corny: A F/F Candy Corn Romance

A True Love Spell Gone Wrong…

A Demon Fairy Godmother?

Her very soul on the line. Can Clover still find true love or is she destined to face the flames alone?

Snuggle: A M/F Demon Teddy Bear Romance

A True Love Spell Gone Wrong…

Jasmine is too busy to go to Hell and she's definitely too busy for demon antics. But when her demon "Fairy Godmother" shows up, everything is on the line. Does she have what it takes to get out of the Devil's bargain or is she doomed to face the flames?

Tangled: A M/F Friends-To-Lovers Sentient Object Romance

A True Love Spell Gone Wrong…

Fern is going to Hell. Not metaphorical Hell but actual, physical Hell. But there's one thing she needs to do before she goes. An item she desperately needs to scratch off the bucket list. And she's hoping the demon sent to guard her will be willing to help her out.

Knotted: A M/F Demon Werewolf Romance

A True Love Spell Gone Wrong…

Violet was no witch but that didn't stop her from trying to use magic to find love. When the spell backfired and left her and her friends bound in a deal with the devil, Violet vowed to find a solution. Now, with less than two months until the deal comes due and zero leads, she's facing the fire. The fire comes early in the form of a great black beast in her bed. Does Violet find the love she's been looking for or does Hell claim her soul?

Light Me Up

He was the first man to ever turn me on. When he flipped my switch and lit me up that first time, I knew he was it for me. There would never be another.

Pounded by the Pommel Horse

Elena loves being on top. When the elite gymnast is challenged to defeat her gym rival on the pommel horse, she's up for the task. But is she up for the ride when the pommel horse shapeshifts into a man? A very, very naked Man?

Christmas with the Monster

He's Got a Package for Her… Devynn expected her first holiday without her kids to be difficult. But nothing could have prepared her for what she found under the tree just after midnight.With the help of his magic sack, the furry, green giant promises Devynn all kinds of pleasure. But would one night with the Christmas monster ever be enough?

Sentient Pen15 from Outer Space

Liam had spent a lot of his childhood obsessed with the legends of the local mines. The abandoned tunnels underground had driven dozens of workers insane and young Liam was desperate to get to the bottom of it. But he found more than he bargained for down there.

Infected by parasitic space mold, Liam has held himself away from relationships for years. When things spark between him and the girl next door, he has no choice but to reveal the truth: his manly appendage is also the bane of his existence.

The Glory Whole Package

Never Piss Off a Witch.

It is a hard-learned lesson and one I may never complete. The endless boredom of my curse is only broken by analyzing the people who use me.

Today I break my silence for the first time and while it might lead to a Happily Ever After, it will never be mine. Not until I've paid for my crimes and earned the forgiveness of the only person I've ever loved.

Getting Railed

"Welcome to Retro Whimsy!"

I hadn't planned on buying anything when entering the new vintage store during my lunch break but somehow found myself leaving with a toy train set.

What could have been written off as an impulse purchase became so much more when those trains come to life.

Now I'm stuck dealing with the consequences of a god curse and deciding if I have what it takes to help break it.